heaven

heaven

ANGELA JOHNSON

Aladdin Paperbacks
New York   London   Toronto   Sydney   Singapore

First Aladdin Paperbacks Edition August 2000

Text copyright © 1998 by Angela Johnson

Aladdin Paperbacks

An imprint of Simon & Schuster Children's Publishing Division

1230 Avenue of the Americas, New York, New York 10020

Designed by Paul Zakris

The text for this book was set in 12-point Garamond 3.

Printed and bound in the United States of America

10 9 8 7 6 5 4 3 2 1

The Library of Congress has cataloged the
hardcover edition as follows:

Johnson, Angela.

Heaven : a novel / by Angela Johnson.—1st ed.

p. cm.

Summary: Fourteen-year-old Marley's seemingly perfect life
in the small town of Heaven is disrupted when she discovers
that her father and mother are not her real parents.

ISBN 0-689-82229-4 (hc.)

[1. Adoption—Fiction. 2. Parent and child—Fiction.
3. Afro-Americans—Fiction.] I. Title.

PZ7.J629He 1998 [Fic]—dc21 98-3291

0-689-82290-1 (Aladdin pbk.)

to kevin

April 28

Sweet Marley,

I'm on my way to Kansas. I guess me and Boy have finished our stay in Oklahoma. I decided on Kansas because of a dream I had. I dream so much now.

How about you? Do you dream of far-away places and the people who live there? Do you dream of the things you have done or might do?

Do you dream of me and Boy?

We dream of you. . . .

We dream and think of you and your family living in the house across from the river. (And yes, before you say anything I happen to know Boy dreams about you. I read him your letters, and he knows who you are. He's an evolved dog.)

About my dream . . .

I'm riding along in my truck and I pass a little boy on the side of the road. He's pointing ahead. I stop the truck and ask him if he needs a ride anywhere, but he just smiles and shakes his head. He keeps pointing, though.

As I ride further down the road, I see you and your mom holding up signs that say KANSAS. *Both of you are wearing long dresses covered in sunflowers–pointing. . . . There's a gentle wind blowing, and your sign blows out of your hand. (Then Boy woke me–he wanted a snack.)*

It was like you were really there, Marley.

Did you dream on the fifteenth of this month?

Maybe you'd dream-skipped to Kansas. . . .

The land of sunflowers and Oz is calling to me. I can't wait to get there. The sunflowers will be in full bloom by the time Boy and I show up.

Boy has decided to change his personality. I'm still checking on the new one. When I truly know what all the changes are–I'll let you know. (But he has become a vegetarian!)

Looks like the oil wells go on forever in Oklahoma . . .

Much love,
Jack and Boy

part one

heaven

*I*n Heaven there are 1,637 steps from my house to the Western Union. You have to walk by a playground and four stores—two clothing, one food, and one hardware coffee shop. After you pass those stores, you cross one street and hop over a deadly looking grate. (I once heard about a man who got struck by lightning while standing on one.) Ten steps past the grate is Ma's Superette.

(If you can't find it at Ma's . . . she even sells live bait on the side.)

Ma's Superette is open 23 1/2 hours a day. Ma closes it from 4:10 A.M. to 4:40 A.M. every morning. She uses the half hour to pray. At least that's what she says she uses it for. When I said differently one day Pops said I was skeptical and not spiritual at all.

That made me mad 'cause hadn't I put all my allowance in the Salvation Army kettle last winter? Sometimes Pops just doesn't get it. He even said a while ago that because I was just fourteen I didn't understand about life, but I wasn't about to hear that. Sometimes he gets so mad at me, he just shakes his head and mumbles that I'm just like Uncle Jack. Then he tosses the thought away I guess and smiles at me, every time.

Anyway, Ma's was the place you could get nachos and nail polish, Levi's when you needed them, and flip-flops for the summer. I'd already gone through two pair and it's only the middle of June.

Heaven might sound pretty boring to most people, but before I really understood about all my years at the Western Union, it was fine for a girl like me.

I don't get sent to Ma's for bread and milk like most kids, but to wire money. I've been doing it ever since I've been allowed to leave the yard by myself. It's something I thought most kids did. It's something I found out a little further down the road that made me different from every other kid in Heaven.

postcards from uncle

We live in Heaven 'cause about twelve years ago Momma found a postcard on a park bench postmarked HEAVEN, OH. On the front of the postcard were clouds and a group of people floating around and waving. It said, HI FROM HEAVEN.

Momma said she'd been looking for Heaven her whole life—so we moved: Momma, Pops, Butchy, and me.

Pops was looking for another job, too. He said it was getting pretty dry out west. Too many people had decided California was the place they had to be. So it was time to go.

But this is how Momma tells it.

"Wasn't much to it. Small town, lots of trees and kids running everywhere. There was the cutest little school sitting over by the river—and when the Impala died right in front of this little house with a picket fence and Marley started screaming to go to the bathroom, we were in Heaven to stay."

Pops says, "What? I don't know. That was ten

or twenty years ago, and how am I supposed to remember any of it? I was almost blind from driving and about out of my mind with sleep. . . . What were we talking about?"

My brother Butchy grunts: "Do I look like the answer man?"

But Momma's telling is only the beginning of how we ended up in Heaven. A postcard, a dead Impala, and a house with a picket fence is only part of what got us here.

Why Momma was looking for Heaven is another thing. People look for what they think they need, I guess. You find what you think you need and what might make you happy in different places with different people and sometimes it's just waiting in a tiny town in Ohio with a cute little schoolhouse by the river. Heaven was waiting for us.

If the whole truth be told, that's adding Pops's truth and the little bit that Butchy knows—I figure we ended up in Heaven because of the postcard, Western Union, and Uncle Jack.

There aren't Western Union offices everywhere, you know. Sometimes you have to go miles to find one. When the car broke down and Pops needed a phone, he had gone to Ma's Superette, called a tow truck, bought bologna sandwiches, and had seen the Western Union sign by the register. Then he'd looked around town and thought maybe it would be a nice place to raise a family and pets.

The story is, between the ages of two and ten I had twelve dogs, fifteen cats, nine rabbits, ten birds (eight being nursed because of cat attacks), one lizard, and 105 goldfish.

Pops say I'm just like his twin brother, Uncle Jack, about animals. It's just not home without something furry or scaly or feathered around. I'm just like Uncle Jack, who's been everywhere in the world and who I only know through letters and the Western Union. . . .

> May 8
> Marley Marley,
> Hey, Angel! How's it going in Heaven?
> If that last hat that I sent you doesn't fit,
> make your melon-headed old man stretch it
> out for you.
> Aren't you a little young for real big hair?
> Although I was about your age when I wore
> my first Afro. Didn't they come back in style
> for a minute?
> Kansas is beautiful. Western Kansas is

*even better than the rest. Last night I slept on
top of my truck. Boy did, too. His tail
wagged all night long. We could see the world
that night.*

*Ever seen a prairie dog, Angel? They're
quick, and Boy got pretty content just sitting
around listening to them at night on top of the
truck.*

*Did you know Kansas has incredible
sunflowers? I'm thinking about hanging
around until they all start to bloom.*

Can you see them, Angel?

*Hundreds of thousands of them waving in
the fields.*

Can you see them, Angel?

*They're tall and languid. Tall and
graceful. They're yellow because they swallow
up the sun and brown in the middle—almost
burnt from eating up all the rays.*

Sunflowers all around . . .

*Plant these seeds in a place Boy might like
to take a nap under.*

*Your uncle Jack (in Kansas)
and Boy*

Uncle Jack hasn't seen me since I was born. He

was in Ohio a few years ago. He said nobody was home for two days. Butchy figures that was the weekend Momma and Pops dragged us to Cleveland to the museums, fireworks, and a rib burn-off.

That was also the weekend Butchy fell off a pier into Lake Erie after visiting the Rock and Roll Hall of Fame. He was playing air guitar and had us all falling on the ground laughing. We got hysterical when he disappeared over the pier until we looked down into the water and saw that Butchy was still playing. He swam to the beach and kept on playing long after Mom had thrown a blanket around him.

Now that's entertainment.

We'd stayed at a hotel downtown (I can't remember the name of it) and had walked around the city most of the first day, counting people wearing Cleveland Indian T-shirts.

We'd even run into a couple of people from Heaven. They were eating ribs at the burn-off in The Flats. (The Flats used to be old warehouses right off the river, but now artists lived in the buildings and festivals were held in the streets.)

Mom and Pops had stood around and talked while Butchy and I stuffed ourselves with elephant ears and french fries. It was a good weekend.

I know it doesn't sound too cool, but I like to hang out with my family. They're a good time.

I wonder what he looks like, my uncle Jack? Pops has one picture of them both. They were in diapers—sitting in a vegetable garden with an old dog at their feet. The writing on the back of the picture says: 1950 THE BOYS AND BOY.

Pops says that he and Uncle Jack have had about eight dogs named Boy. That makes Boy part of the circle, just like the rest of us are, but some of us are just finding out what our part is.

shadow ghosts and cadillacs

Shoogy Maple sees shadow ghosts and had been kicked out of every school she'd gone to. Then she moved to Heaven. Her family moved in across the playground last year.

Shoogy wears frosted lipstick and cutoff T-shirts (even in the winter) and knee-high rain boots wherever she goes; and she mostly goes with me.

We met at Ma's. She was buying a Slurpee and a burrito and putting money in a can to help rebuild churches that had been burned in the south. I was wiring money to Uncle Jack somewhere in Utah and wondering if Ma would let me use her bathroom.

Shoogy started scooping the beans out of her burrito and feeding them to Ma's cat, who was standing in the bin of flip-flops.

Ma grinned at her and went over to do the paperwork on my wiring.

I scratched the cat's head.

Shoogy said, "I like this cat. She's not afraid to

mooch. Most cats will just look at you like you're trying to feed them poison."

Not Ma's cat. She'd break into your house and drag the refrigerator across the lawn if she could.

This cat was notorious in the neighborhood for being the biggest beggar in the business district. Everyone fed her, and she was so fat, I didn't know how she'd managed to hop into the flip-flop bin.

When I said this to Shoogy, she howled so hard that she dropped her Slurpee.

Ma shook her head, put a roll of paper towels on the counter, and I helped the laughing girl clean cherry Slurpee off the floor. And when the cat started fighting us for the last of the Slurpee we both started laughing and screaming.

In the end we all got kicked out—cat included. On the bench outside of Ma's we introduced ourselves and laughed till our stomachs hurt.

I'd liked Shoogy on the spot.

Anyway—that's how we met. The reason we became and stayed friends was that she wasn't like anybody in her family and like everybody in mine.

Shoogy thinks the stupidest things are funny. She buys the worst tabloid papers (aren't all of them the worst?) looking for alien abduction stories, then has hours of conversation with my mom and dad about them.

My parents love it.

Shoogy says she can't share her alien theories with her parents. They get wrinkles in their foreheads and smile like they're in pain.

I guess the Maples are pretty dry.

Pops says that you shouldn't judge people too harsh, but I could sit all day in the middle of the street judging Shoogy's family and not get tired.

The Maples are "too" beautiful for Heaven.

They all have perfect heads and perfect teeth. There are two boys. Perfect. Two girls (off to camp tomorrow)—besides Shoogy. Perfect. And two perfect parents that smiled at everybody like mannequins and kept the most perfect yard in town.

Heaven is a pink flamingo, woolly sheep in the front yard kind of place. . . .

But the Maples got landscapers and awed everybody on Center Street. I'm pretty sure I was the only person in the whole town who judged them, though. You can pretty much do what you want around here and nobody says anything.

And then there was the way Shoogy acted when her family was around. . . .

Like a few months ago in March. Shoogy and me were hanging out of the tree in her front yard when her family pulled up in a brand-new car.

Shoogy said under her breath, "They went and did it again."

Then she somersaulted out of the tree and stood in front of the car with her hands in her pockets and her rain boots dug in.

I'm still hanging from the tree and thinking the big new car is pretty cool—considering it probably depletes half the region's fossil fuel, like our Impala does—until Shoogy kicks at the front of the grill and stomps down the street.

Six perfect Maple heads turn and watch her go.

I'm surprised at Shoogy. Surprised and worried a little about why a dumb car could make her so mad.

It was a couple of days after kicking the Cadillac that Shoogy started seeing the shadow ghost behind Pops. She said if you just glanced at the ghost, you'd think you were having double vision. But . . . if you stared at it for a while, it became a shadow with a warm glow. Following Pops.

Over and over Shoogy described the shadow, but I never saw it. That seemed to really get on

Shoogy's nerves. Shoogy said she had never seen a ghost before. She blamed it on living in a town called Heaven.

I blamed it on her being overheated wearing those rain boots all the time.

But even Pops's shadow ghost didn't keep Shoogy from still hating the green Cadillac. I sat in the car one morning while Mr. Maple beamed at the side of it. It looked like an airplane inside, and the seats felt better than the first-class airline seats I sneaked into once on a trip to New Mexico.

Mr. Maple said, "She's a beaut."

I nodded my head and looked across the yard at Shoogy as I reclined the automatic seats. You'd have thought I was drowning puppies by the way she looked at me.

Shoot! Not too many people in Heaven had automatically reclining seats in their cars. I'm pretty sure those seats made Shoogy hate the car even more. In her mind it didn't belong here. I don't think she thought her beautiful family did, either.

"What were you doing when you were eight, Marley?"

Shoogy and me were sitting on the sliding board and not letting any little kids go down it.

"I don't know; getting on Butchy's nerves and going to second grade, I guess."

Shoogy lifted her leg from the slide like she'd been burned. She took off her boots and tossed them under the slide, then she gave the little kids playing a nasty look—daring them to touch.

Shoogy says, "When I was eight, I was in beauty contests."

"Beauty contests?"

"Yeah. Why not?"

Shoogy got up and walked up and down the slide like she had a book on her head. Her frosted lipstick sparkled in the sunlight.

She has a drawer full of frosted lipstick.

"I used to walk like this, then like this."

Shoogy puts her hands on her hips and struts up and down the sliding board. She puts a fake smile on her face and blows kisses to all the kids on the playground. The way she walks the slide, her cut-offs and T-shirt could be a ball dress. Then it came to me—under that old wool hat and behind those dark plastic sunglasses, Shoogy Maple was beautiful.

I don't trust her family now. Something isn't

right with all that perfection.

It makes me wonder why Shoogy stopped being beautiful and started hating Cadillacs.

Uncle Jack came up with a list of code words for giving the Western Union—he says he prefers them and that they work better for him. Says he doesn't want to carry a picture ID around in his pocket. He says he's lost so many wallets, he can't count them. (He leaves them on diner counters and in rest rooms.) So he gave each day of the week a special word. If money is wired on a certain day of the week, he uses that code word to pick it up. No need for a driver's license picture. The words:

> Monday—Sacrifice
> Tuesday—Truth
> Wednesday—Power
> Thursday—Beauty
> Friday—Life
> Saturday—Memory
> Sunday—Obedience

I had them memorized by the time I was six. The words I didn't understand Momma explained to me.

I wonder what Ma at the Superette thought of me then, my note from Pops allowing me to wire the money, and the way I recited the word. I stood on tiptoe looking at the jawbreakers next to the register, hoping Ma wouldn't forget to give me one. She never did.

Uncle Jack's words.

That's all I know of him. His letters and the words he's lent to us to be a part of him.

Sometimes after I'd left the Superette, I'd lean next to the outside wall and imagine my uncle Jack. If I closed my eyes at the right moment I could see him.

Sometimes he's a grown man on a lonely country road writing on a piece of paper. Other times he's the shadowy baby in the picture surrounded by vegetables, his brother, and his old dog.

Mostly, though, Uncle Jack is just shadowy.

to the amish

Sometimes when Bobby Morris's car is working and his baby Feather is awake and not cranky, we take off to the Amish.

It's one of my favorite places.

Bobby once said that if it wasn't for Pennsylvania he'd only be forty minutes from Brooklyn. He'd be able to live in Heaven, and still visit what he used to know.

Bobby says he's always felt kind of Amish— kind of isolated from everyone, moving around at a different pace. The Amish have got each other, though. And Bobby's got Feather.

Feeling kind of Amish with Bobby and Feather is always a good time for me and Shoogy when Heaven isn't enough.

It's the greenest grass along Route 608, and the car rolls along with Feather in her car seat singing to the radio. We know when we get to Middlefield because Bobby always turns the radio off and rolls down his window. The smells are sweet cut grass, farmyards, and horses. . . .

⌒

Bobby lives over Canvas—they frame stuff, and I don't know how they make any money in Heaven, but they've been there for years. Anyway, Canvas beats the car repair shop Bobby used to live next door to. Here it's quiet and bikers don't come around there to drink beer and rev their engines at 1:30 in the morning.

Bobby put a flier up last winter at Ma's looking for a baby-sitter. What the flier said was:

LOOKING FOR A DEPENDABLE, BABY-FRIENDLY
PERSON. REFERENCES. TRANSPORTATION.
MUST KNOW "YOU ARE MY SUNSHINE"
AND LIKE *Sesame Street.*

The flier was purple with a pencil drawing of Feather in a diaper. Bobby says me and a woman named Trudy (who smoked like a chimney and asked him if Feather minded a little noise, 'cause she bowled four times a week at the Pro-Lane Alley in the mornings) were up for the job.

I started watching Feather the second week of vacation.

Feather was easy to fall in love with. The first

time I saw her, Bobby was holding her and greeting me with a peace sign. They were surrounded by walls the same purple as the flier. Feather looked like her picture, tiny with wispy hair and caramel skin. A feather. Bobby and her mom must have named her after they met for the first time.

The purple walls made me feel at home, and Shoogy felt the same way after she'd come in off the steps to meet Bobby and Feather. Momma had Shoogy come along in case Bobby turned out to be a kidnapper.

That's Bobby, and even though he has purple walls he says that plain and simple are always the best. That's why he likes Route 608. The smells and the sights.

Plain and simple.

"Feather likes rhubarb pie more than almost anything," Bobby says.

She proves it by trying to shove a whole piece into her mouth. She's eating the pie and calling the cows that surround us "kitties" and "dogs."

"It looks it," Shoogy says, then wipes blueberries off her rain boots and lies back in the grass.

As far as you can see there's nothing but grass and barns. We sit in our favorite field next to an old barn that looks like it's been deserted for a hundred years. It holds nothing to feed the cows and it doesn't look like it'll stand up to the next rain.

Furniture stores all over Ohio have been taking the old barns and making chests, tables, and bookshelves from them. Everybody's advertising "reclaimed barn wood."

There's enough falling-down barns in Ohio to put furniture in every house in this part of the state.

Bobby licks his fingers and Feather's, too—'cause he has no choice when she sticks them into his mouth as she crawls over him to go after some dandelions she's spotted.

Bobby moans, "She likes dandelions almost as much as rhubarb pie."

We watch her as she hides the butter-yellow weeds in her pull-up diapers.

Bobby finishes up his pie and says, "She looks like her mother."

"Did she eat flowers, too?" I ask.

Bobby adjusts his glasses on his nose and smiles. "No, but she was one." Then he looks at Feather as if she is the only baby in the whole world. Sometimes I catch Momma looking at me and Butchy that way. But Bobby never talks about Feather's mom.

The two people I like most—outside my family—have secrets that I don't ask about. Momma says it's a flaw. She says I should be more interested; that people like to be asked about themselves. I should find out what made them who they are.

I look at Shoogy and Bobby and think it doesn't matter 'cause the past doesn't always make sense of the present.

Sometimes Shoogy drops hints about what she did before her family moved to Heaven. But Bobby never says anything. It looks to me like you're either born in Heaven or you come here from someplace else to start all over and forget what happened before.

Across the road four Amish women in dark blue dresses push mowers to cut their yards. They mow back and forth in their dresses, black stockings, and white caps. We all watch, and they don't seem to notice that we're even there. Even Feather stops picking dandelions. A cow moos off in the distance and Bobby reaches over and picks Feather up.

She squirms out of his arms, dashes as fast as her little legs can carry her, falls, then gets up and starts running and pointing again, this time to the women mowing the grass.

The sound of the push mowers echoes on the hot June evening and the only other sound is the occasional cow and car passing on the road.

It's almost perfect.

Feather stops running and pointing and turns around to start pointing at her dad. Bobby is to her in ten strides.

He says, "It's almost like a movie. It's so perfect."

Feather eats a dandelion and says, "Perfect."

letter from uncle

May 24

Marley,

Yesterday I met a man whose father was a
cowboy in the early 1900s. He died when the
man was just four years old, in a riding
accident. The man says what he remembers
most about his father was the sound of his
voice. Can you imagine that? Can you
imagine remembering a voice from a hundred
years ago. The man says he couldn't remember
what his father looked like, but he could
remember the voice that talked him into riding
his first horse and taught him how to write
his name.

I was sitting along a lake yesterday trying
to recollect if I could remember the voices of
people who were gone. I surprised myself. I
actually heard some—well, a couple, really.

I remember the voice of the man who saved
my life by dragging me out of a Vietnamese

river. I had never met him before. He died going back into the river for somebody else. I remember he kept saying that everything was going to be just fine. He kept saying, "Just fine, man, just fine."

Anyway, I've started hearing that voice again, and that's almost been thirty years.

Can you even imagine thirty years, Marley?

Can you imagine even twenty. I couldn't at your age 'cause twenty was an age I never thought I'd see. But that's all tied up in the voices, too.

How is Heaven and your family in it?

I like the picture you sent me of your friends in the field of cows. Those were cows, weren't they? I think that your friends must be interesting people. The kind that I would like to know.

Do any one of them practice a form of ancestor worship? I only ask because that baby looks like she's been around the world before. A very old soul.

I believe that Boy may be getting old. He's not slowing down or anything like that. It's just that he no longer looks at people or other *animals like a young dog would. He seems to judge a situation or person before getting involved.*

I mean—I taught this dog to be trusting of people. It's always worked before. Now he looks at me like I'm two years old, as if to say—let me handle this.

Such is life.

I've been thinking lately that I should maybe settle down and stay in one place for more than a few months. (Don't tell your dad.) I saw this family the other day that looked so happy. They were sitting on the side of the road eating ice cream. They'd pulled a quilt out and just sort of took over the area by the parked car as a picnic spot.

They laughed and waved to passing cars and had themselves a good old time and I thought—me and Boy do that every day. What must it be like to go home to a house that you've lived in and bought things for. Things you love surrounded by the people you love.

Anyway, all that just made me think of you all—so I decided to write. And what with Boy acting a little standoffish with the world. . . .

Oh, yeah, to answer the questions from your last letter.

The picture I sent you was of a dinosaur, hot-dog stand. Good dogs, too. There's a whole town of dinosaurs and things like that in Arizona. You should see it. Little kids almost can't stand it. They get so happy.

Yeah, I play the guitar well. I know it looks good in pictures, but I can truly play it. Doesn't your dad still play his? We learned together. He was always better at it than me.

And yes, one day I will just show up in Heaven and surprise all of you. I mean, what fun would that be? You get so few happy surprises in life. . . .

Let my coming there out of the blue be one that you won't forget until I'm way gone out the front door. Love to your dad, mom, brother, and anyone who means anything to you.

Your uncle Jack
and Boy

hitching

*Y*esterday Bobby picked this man up about four miles outside of town.

Momma said, "He must be crazy giving rides to strangers the way the world is today."

Then she mumbles something about what kids don't ever think will happen, but she grins and winks at me.

"Don't hitch, my girl. Okay?"

I grin back at her.

Hitching.

Most people in Heaven think that anyone who doesn't live here must have something wrong with them. It doesn't interest many of them what other people do outside of town, but when new people move in and get settled, they can basically do no wrong in the eyes of Heaven.

So as I'm pushing Feather down the sidewalk to the park, I'm thinking how the people I hang around with have been here less than a year, and they fit into Heaven just fine. And even while I don't know what I'd do without Shoogy and

Bobby, they sure aren't the people next door.

They're the kind of people who'd hitch to somewhere like the Natural History Museum and look at the stuffed animals, or to the Arcade to shop.

I take Feather out of her stroller and put her in the sandbox by the baby swings. The first thing she does is grab two handfuls of sand and pour them both over her head. I notice that the rest of the kids in the sandbox have the same beige covering their heads, so I figure as long as none got in her eyes she'll be okay.

I sit next to the sandbox and read a book about Montana.

"Nice baby."

I look up and smile at a woman sitting on the bench nearby.

I say, "Yeah, she is a nice baby."

"You baby-sitting?"

"Yeah."

"Do you watch other kids?"

"No, but do you need a sitter for your kids?"

She shrugs and waves to the sandbox when one of the kids stands up and shakes about fifty pounds of sand off himself. He runs over to us and leans against the woman.

She doesn't seem to mind that he's covering her blue business suit with sand. She smiles off into nowhere and rubs the little boy's back until he toddles back to the others.

I look up every thirty seconds to check on Feather, and by the time I'm on my way to freezing to death with the woman in Montana it's time to go. The woman in the blue has already left with her little boy.

I figure no more reading at the park. Feather could have gone up the street and robbed a store or something in the few seconds my eyes are on my book. I don't think Bobby would be too happy. Parents in general are a nervous group.

I notice it in my own parents and strangers, too. It's like these kids are either bombs or precious gems to them. I don't think they know whether to cover them in something soft and keep them close, or just watch them carefully, making sure they don't do too much damage to the world around them.

Bobby has that cover-them-in-a-soft-blanket thing going on. . . .

Feather likes to fly, so I strap her into her stroller, surround her with pillows, and push her around the deserted parking lot by the feed mill like a crazy person. She loves it. In between screaming laughs she throws her head back and claps.

I stroll her back to my house, where we eat and wear most of her food. We look at all the commercials on TV. Feather loves any commercial with music in it.

By the time Bobby's car is pulling up in front of the house, Feather and me have had enough commercials and have pulled every dandelion there ever was in our yard. We have eight jelly jars full of them.

Feather starts pumping her arms up and down when she sees Bobby. He picks her up, smells and kisses the top of her head, and smiles.

"How's she been today?"

"Fine. I think she's been talking."

"What's she been saying?"

I hand Bobby a jar of dandelions and like his smell. He smells like paint and oranges.

"Oh, just baby things."

Bobby holds Feather and the dandelions close to him, and I start to see the resemblance. Feather still has a baby face that could change any time, but she already has Bobby's mouth and ears.

Feather turns to me and gives me her baby

tooth smile, presses her face against Bobby's shirt, and falls to sleep in no time at all.

As I watch Feather with Bobby I have a picture in my mind of Pops and me washing his car. I must be about three years old. I'm making a big mess rather than helping, but Pops keeps smiling and letting me put soap back on rinsed parts of the car.

He just keeps rinsing and smiling. . . .

I ask Bobby if he's picked up any more hitchers.

He calls to me over his shoulder as he walks away. "Not today, but you never know what's gonna come down in Heaven."

part two

burning dark

Down south they're burning churches. Pops says it reminds him of the early sixties. He says, "Mississippi," in a whisper and goes out back, sits on a lawn chair near the big old maple tree, and listens to the crickets.

That's what Pops does when he's about had it. Cricket listening.

Momma told me last week that they burnt down the church in Alabama that Pops and I went to when we were babies. She saw it burn on the news. She looked at me like she was going to tell me something, but stopped herself. She didn't mention that she'd ever been in the church. I thought that was weird.

Me and Butchy sit in front of the TV and watch another church fall down in flames. Flames that I can feel sitting a thousand miles away. Flames that I will feel long after the TV is turned off. Flames and the looks on the faces of people watching their churches burn down—burning hot into the night, burning dark when the morning comes up.

Butchy moves close to me. "They won't burn churches here, will they?"

I don't say anything. I look at him and see he's pretty scared about the fires. He moves off slowly to the back kitchen door like Daddy did. I'm left with the TV and Momma.

Momma crosses her legs and cracks her gum at the screen. She could stare anybody scared with the look she's giving.

"There's always going to be sick people, I guess."

Momma starts swinging her foot like she always does when she gets mad. That's the only way you know she's upset. Her foot swinging.

"But why churches now?" she asks like she's figuring out a math problem. I watch her like she might really know, like she has to know. I can't ask her, though. She might answer her questions, and I don't know if I want to know that much yet, but I got a feeling I don't have much to say concerning what I learn about the world.

Ethel Grabski always has our mail in the box by 1:30, every day. She's better than a clock as she hikes up the sidewalk in good walking shoes and the mailbag hung over her shoulder. She's been bringing us mail since I can remember. All five foot and beehive hairdo of hers. She smiles and wears what she calls blood red sea lipstick. She hands me the mail and stalks toward the next house.

Two letters for Pops and one for Momma, and a letter for somebody named Monna Floyd in care of Momma and Pops. I hand the mail to Momma while she talks on the phone about dry cleaning, then walk through the living room to my bedroom.

I don't ever remember Momma mentioning anybody named Monna Floyd. Stuff like this gives me what Pops calls the "nosies." I make sure I read the names and addresses of most of the personal letters that come to the house. (Just a thing I have, even though most of the time I feel like other people's lives aren't anybody's business.)

It's funny how you sometimes don't realize when you might be doing something for the last time. I didn't know it then, but that would be my last walk to my bedroom knowing anything about who I was.

I asked Bobby once what it was like to know Feather was really his, came from him, and was the closest person in the world to him.

He said it was important, of course, that she came from him, but people made too much of that kind of thing. They just did.

He was holding Feather's hand and kissing it.

He's one of those people who always says things like that. Somehow, though, I know he believes it. Even while kissing Feather's hand—I know he believes it.

It's a couple of hours later and I'm still thinking about Monna Floyd and churches burning down. I wonder if the Alabama-postmarked letter is from someone who's seen the burnings firsthand. It's like that six degrees of separation thing . . . everybody is closer than they think to everybody else.

I listen to the television as I hang over the side of my bed. The newscaster keeps going on about what a tragedy it all is—the church burnings. He also talks about how some of the burnings could be copycats.

I think it's a stupid thing to say. Burning something down for any reason is disgusting enough to stand on its own and not be thought of as something that's being repeated 'cause the idea was good.

A sweet wind blows in through my window,

and I can smell the honeysuckle. The sheer curtains float over my head, and I am just about to fall into a nap. Momma says I used to fight them when I was little. I'd stand straight up on my bed and refuse to sleep.

I guess naps are something some of us have to grow into. I remember thinking this as the smell of honeysuckle and the feel of smooth silky window curtains across my face, took me away.

If I dreamed in my nap I don't remember any of it. It was just a sweet summer sleep. I love the way I feel after a nap. I like that it's still day and I can hear Momma and Pops talking and the ice-cream truck coming down the street. Momma's and Pops's voices almost put me back to sleep until I hear Pops's voice raise.

I lay there until I hear the screen door close. I look out my window to see Momma sitting next to Pops. She's holding a piece of paper. Her head leans against his, and her eyes are closed. She soon lets the paper blow away. Pops gets up and follows it, reads it, and slowly looks up toward my window.

I wave and turn away and think how tall Pops is and how funny he looked stooping to pick up the paper.

storm

The sun is scorching when Momma comes into my room and lays down next to me on the bed. Her feet and legs hang over most of it.

"Do you think you might get out of this room before nightfall?"

"I had a good nap and woke up a long time ago. I just don't want to get up. The air is smelling so good here."

"The air always smells good here."

I roll on my side and look at Momma's face.

She has what Pops calls a classic face. Momma says that means she's not ugly or beautiful, just classic. I like that. I want to be classic like Momma.

Shoogy's beautiful. My brother Butchy's beautiful. I'm not jealous or anything. I'm okay about me. I've got a good face.

I touch the side of Momma's face and move a wisp of hair behind her ear. She just stares at me, then smiles.

She jumps up and heads for the door. "Get up,

Marley—it's almost time to eat."

I watch Momma head for the door, then roll over on my back. She stops at the door and opens her mouth to say something, but nothing comes out. It scares me for a second, but she smiles and moves quietly out the door. The sheers blow across my face again.

It wasn't the storm, and it wasn't just that Butchy was supposed to come home and hadn't.

(My brother is two years younger and five inches taller than me. He hates organized sports and anything having to do with school. He says he'd be happy just to stay at his computer checking out the astrophysics Web site and hanging out at Junior's parking lot skateboarding with his friends.)

It wasn't even that Pops forgot about the fish cooking on the grill and let it burn, either.

It was everything.

It was one of those nights that started to go down before the sun did.

Me, Momma, and Pops end up eating hot dogs at the picnic table. Nobody's smiling by that time. Momma is trying to hide that she's staring at me, but Pops isn't hiding it at all.

I finally get sick of it and in the middle of a mouth full of relish and onions, I stick out my tongue at both of them. It works most times. Usually Momma tells me it's gross, and Pops shakes his head and tells me to keep my tongue in my head.

This time nobody says anything.

They just swat flies and keep on eating.

I say, "Guess I'll run uptown to see what Bobby is doing."

Pops says, "Uh-no."

"Why?"

"Because it's going to storm."

He looks up when he says it, and I notice the sky is a funny yellow color.

"I'll be back before it does. I swear."

When I get up to leave, Momma reaches across the table and grabs my arm.

"We said no."

I sit down and say, "Hell," under my breath.

"What?" Momma says.

"Nothing," I say, looking up at the yellow sky and sideways at Momma and Pops.

It isn't just the storm.

Oh yeah, it makes sense that we're in the basement

now. The wind is knocking over lawn chairs and blowing the bushes around the side of the house.

The radio is saying a funnel cloud touched down over Middlefield, and I worry that the Amish don't have radios. I worry that they don't know what's coming at them. I worry that it's not fair and I can't do anything about it.

I sit next to Pops on the big cushy couch that's losing its stuffing. Anything losing its stuffing or missing a leg ends up in the basement rec room. I love it down here. Everything's comfortable and cozy.

Momma is sitting on the beanbag, as close to the radio as she can be. I guess it makes her feel better to be able to turn the volume up or down. I know she's thinking about Butchy, she's thinking about all the ways she can make his life miserable for worrying her during a tornado.

I don't want to think about it and fall off to sleep.

Pops wakes me. It's lightning out. I see it through the glass-block basement windows. I feel even sleepier, but I know something is wrong.

Momma gets off the beanbag and comes to sit on the other side of me, then I lean against her. All I can think about during the storm is the song

"The Itsy-Bitsy Spider." It keeps going through my head.

Pops says, "Momma and me want to talk to you about something."

Down came the rain and washed the spider out.

Down came the rain and washed the spider out.

I remember later that night what Bobby told me. That the Amish trust nature to tell them when a tornado is coming. They trust the air around them and the way their animals behave. They watch the way the leaves blow and how the sky looks and the air feels. They trust nature to tell them what the man on the radio tells us.

I like that kind of faith.

I could have that kind of faith—in nature.

I now know how to watch for the danger signs, and I will from now on.

time

There's this movie where a man thinks he's the only human left on the earth. But he keeps living like he did when the world was full of people. He won't change. It's like, if his life changes at all, he'll have to look around and see the real reason why all the other people are dead.

I always watch that movie when it comes on. I always feel sorry for the man, too—every time.

Last night Momma and Pops kept saying that they should have told me what they had to tell me sooner. It's what people who haven't told the truth always say. From now on when I want to say something—I say it then. It's easier, and you won't have to think about it later.

It's strange how I couldn't take my mind off that letter and those church burnings. I'm thinking it started with Ethel Grabski delivering the mail yesterday, but I guess it started a long time ago.

July 20, 1996
Lucy & Kevin Carroll
34 Riverview Rd.
Heaven, OH 00127

Dear Mr. & Mrs. Carroll,

   I received your address from a distant relative of Mr. Carroll's here in Alabama. She was kind enough to pass it on to my wife, Pastor Anna Major.

   I write this letter bearing sad news. It is news that many congregations here in the south have been enduring.

   Our First Mission Church was burned last week. It is a very dark time for us all.

   Even with all this chaos I am in the process of trying to re-create some of our files that were badly damaged. Sadly, your niece Monna Floyd's baptismal records were in the latter. I would be grateful if you could send us a good quality photocopy of the original certificate. As Monna's mother, Christine, is dead, and her father, Jack Raymond Carroll, is impossible to find, I hope that you have these records.

   We were so very fortunate that I could

*re-create actual dates of baptisms, weddings,
and so forth from my wife's daily diaries that
span some twenty years, and that this diary
was in our home at the time of the fire.*

I hope that you can help us.
May God smile on you.
Deacon James David Major

And that was it.

Momma and Pops let me read it after telling it
all. I almost felt the heat of the flames, flickering
and scorching me way up here in Ohio.

When it was safe to come out of the basement, I
walked up the stairs into a whole new house.
Nothing looked or felt the same. I didn't have a
place anymore.

I was like one of those people who gets hit
on the head and doesn't remember anything,
except past events kept coming to me, then disap-
pearing again. They kept flying out of the pictures
and furniture.

I caught glimpses of two summers ago when I
was having a water fight with Mom and Butchy. I
had a flash of Pops falling off the ladder while painting the house and covering the shrubs with paint.

I saw me as a little kid again, washing the car with Pops, and him smiling . . .

Nothing belonged to me anymore.

Momma and Pops had held my hand and told me the story in quiet voices and with sad, teary eyes. They'd said the right things and looked the right way while they were telling.

I stared at my hands and kept thinking, I thought I had my Momma's hands, and I probably did. It was just a different momma, one buried way down south in the cool red dirt of Alabama.

I want to see the movie about the man who refuses to change, soon. I guess I could rent it.

Maybe the man knew what made sense all the time.

I'd felt sorry for him because he didn't understand time. It moved on, but he didn't. He held on to a place in time that was gone. That's the thing about time—it's always long gone.

I didn't understand what the man in the movie did, that changes can drag you somewhere you didn't want to go. . . .

more shadow ghosts

It's been two weeks, and I still have not cried.

I decided while walking along the river, that the shadows Shoogy saw around my Pops—or uncle, or whatever—was a wraith. It followed him 'cause it knew what was coming. Maybe it was there to punish him for what he did and for what was about to come out.

It wasn't just a shadow ghost after all.

"Do you want spaghetti, Marley?"

Shoogy's house is all cream-colored walls and air that smells like apples. Fresh and clean. The kitchen sparkles until we show up and start making food. I have a feeling every room in the house sparkles until Shoogy makes an entrance.

Mrs. Maple wears a white tennis dress and smiles like a doll. She has perfect hair.

I nod my head about the spaghetti and watch the way Mrs. Maple smiles as Shoogy spills a jar of spaghetti sauce all over the counter.

Shoogy screams, "I got it," and smears the counter even more.

Mrs. Maple kisses Shoogy on the head and walks smiling out the kitchen with a tennis racket.

I say, "Your mom's nice."

Shoogy licks her sauce-covered elbow.

"Yeah, she's real nice. Always has been nice. Always will be nice."

"Nothing wrong with that," I say, meaning it.

Shoogy smirks at me with her frosted lips.

Past Ma's Superette and across the street from the bike shop there is a little alley that the town blocked off and put in some benches and flowers. They let the kids in the town grafitti the walls surrounding the garden. You'd think something like that would be ugly, but it's not. I think it's one of the most beautiful places in Heaven.

The walls get painted over once a month.

Everybody used to spray paint the overpass going out of town, and the city council thought this would be an alternative. It mostly is. Some stuff still gets tagged on the overpass—but I don't think the sprayers really put their hearts into it anymore.

Bobby is standing in the shadow of the left wall using a paintbrush. Feather sits at his feet making baby noises and pulling off her polka-dot socks.

Bobby doesn't turn around as I pick Feather up and take her to a bench. I smell her sweet baby hair.

"You ever think about using spray paint, Bobby?"

Bobby's brown legs are paint covered, and you can't tell where they end or his dark khaki shorts begin. He wears one of those safari hats 'cause he thinks it's funny. It is.

Bobby says, "Can't control the medium out of the can."

"Did you ever try?"

"Oh yeah." He laughs, turning around and looking at the opposite wall, then at me and Feather. "I was arrested in Brooklyn for it. I'm not fast enough for that kind of art."

"Was it real bad?"

"What, getting arrested or what I painted on the wall?"

Feather pulls my hair and tries to get down to get a bug. I let her.

"Getting arrested. I'd freak."

Bobby stops painting and turns around, smiles

and starts painting again. "I did freak. Feather was with a neighbor and she was definitely the type to punch 911 if I was late. Bad night."

"Some life," I say.

Bobby doesn't say anything else, and I watch him. He's painted over half the wall with black paint. He's not leaving it to the city.

I get on the ground and crawl around with Feather. She's managed to put a few things in her mouth while I'm talking to Bobby. She smiles and clamps her mouth shut when I try to open it.

Feather goes into a fast crawl to get away, then turns around and gives me the look Bobby always does when he is about to say something funny.

I remember looking at my hands and realizing that they weren't Momma's hands.

It would never be as simple for us as it is with Bobby and Feather.

I start to cry.

armed

$\mathcal{B}$obby's arms are strong, and he holds me in them for a long time. Feather holds on to my feet and drools a little. Yesterday I told him everything. He fixed me soup.

Now he keeps saying, "Just think about today."

Bobby comes from what he calls a twelve-step background. He always takes everything one day at a time. He says tomorrow will come whether we're here or not.

So I try. . . .

I think only about today and how Butchy kept pounding on the bathroom door trying to get me to come out and the way he looked when he saw me walking up behind him after I'd climbed out the window. Then I try to only think about when Momma tried to talk to me and Pops tried to back her up and I only said, "Hell," and walked away.

I think of today when I walked by the river and thought about my father—Jack.

I just try to think of today, and Bobby's arms. . . .

⌒

Bobby says it's like this. . . .

You're this little kid and the first thing you remember is dropping a toy. Then somebody picks it up for you. Hey! It's that nice woman who comes when you scream or the funny man who throws you in the air and lets you eat the things the woman frowns at.

Then you know who they are.

Then you *think* they know who you are.

You do something stupid, they fix it. You're a kid, and they're the parents.

"Anyway," Bobby says, "it's just a matter of time before they get caught doing something stupid."

I say, "Bobby, this ain't funny."

He holds me tighter.

"It's not funny."

He holds me so tight, I can hardly breathe— then I start laughing. I laugh until I'm on my back in the alley.

Blue sky above and black wall tunneling up.

Feather crawls toward Bobby, gets within a foot of him, then curls up in the cool sand and goes to sleep.

⌒

"I hate them, Bobby."

Bobby takes off his paint-spattered shirt and covers Feather with it.

"Must be hard to hate people you've loved for most of your life."

I get up and walk over to the black shiny wall. He's started a painting. It's going to be a slow, steady painting. Bobby's going to take his time. He says that he once worked on a painting for a year and changed it about twenty times. He had to put it away.

I lean against the black wall.

"Happening wall, Bobby."

Bobby says quieter, "Must be hard to hate people you've loved. . . ."

I turn to face the wall. "For most of my life."

Bobby lifts up Feather, who keeps sleeping.

I look at Bobby holding Feather and decide to leave.

"Later," Bobby says.

I run from the alley and head to Ma's.

I buy three purple pair of flip-flops, three different sizes, and head out into the light.

I drop a pair off at Shoogy's. I leave them with the twin boys, who are polite and say they will give them to her when she gets home from fishing.

I say, "Fishing?"

They say, "Yes, fishing," and smile at me.

I drop off Bobby's flip-flops at his door. I sit a while on the steps and watch people go in and out of Canvas, then leave when the sun starts going down.

Momma is digging in the front yard as I come up the sidewalk. She pulls her gloves off and waves me over. "Marley, baby, time to talk."

I stand in front of her, but don't say a thing. There's nothing more to say. Momma and Pops are my aunt and uncle and Jack. . . .

I don't have to say anything. I guess she sees I know it all in my eyes.

Momma stands up and puts her hands on her hips. I've seen her do that so many times, but this time is like the first time. I wonder how many other things will seem like the first time now. I keep moving down the walk into the house.

Momma doesn't stop me.

I go looking around the house for Butchy and finally find him in Momma and Pops's closet. I only see his feet as I walk into the room. He's buried his head way underneath a pile of sweaters that used to be folded and packed neatly. Sweaters are everywhere now.

I sit on the bed and wait for him to finish looking for what he wants in the closet.

The sweaters fall away around Butchy as he pulls out the metal box Momma and Pops keep all their important papers in. Then he looks up and sees me for the first time.

"What's up, brother?"

Butchy opens the box and starts going through the papers. He finds what he wants, looks at it for a minute—then puts it back in the box and shoves it in the closet. He hops up on the bed and sits beside me.

"What were you looking for?"

He puts his arm around me and looks at the closet. "Just making sure, I guess."

"Are you theirs?"

He slides off the bed and heads for the door. "Yeah, I guess so. But it's better to be armed with the truth, you know?"

I look at the mess in the closet and leave the room and just try to think about today.

dreams

I used to dream that a witch came through my window at night, walked over to my bed, grabbed me, and put me on the back of her broom. She'd fly down the stairs and head out the door with me. I'd always wake up screaming, only I'd never make a noise. Every time, though, Pops would be kneeling beside my bed, telling me the witch was gone.

He knew it, you know. I heard him tell Momma once. He knew the exact moment to wake up and go to me. I was so glad when I grew out of that dream, even though I missed Pops taking me downstairs and giving me a spoonful of peanut butter.

I miss that, but not the dreams.

I used to write my uncle Jack about my dreams, and he said he had a book that could explain all the dreams in the world. I thought that was it! A book to explain all the good and bad dreams. . . .

You can smell the water before you get to it, and all the houses look like little beach shacks. Lake Erie is close.

I turn and look in the backseat, and Shoogy is feeding Feather Cheerios and singing off-key to opera from the radio.

Bobby nods his head to an imaginary beat and lets about a million people cut in front of us when we get to Mentor-on-the-Lake. He calls it Zen driving, and we're all used to it.

We find the noisiest and most crowded place on the beach to put our blanket down. Little sticky kids run crazy on the sand. About seven different radio stations are being played from different parts of the beach. Sunblock, Kool-Aid, and all different-colored coolers remind me why I've always loved coming here.

Me and Boy have been on the road so long, we feel like part of the pickup truck.

Boy sits up on the front seat and barks at all the cows that we pass. He barks at cows, horses and, about ten miles back, at a truckload of chickens parked in a diner lot. Boy just wants some buddies. There's no meanness in him when he barks.

Seems like we've been driving down this road for days. There are no hills and, for that matter, not too many things to sit on top of a hill.

Suddenly, though, out of nowhere—to the left
side of the road—there's a huge lake. Umbrellas
and little kids running around—probably
ignoring their parents—were everywhere. Boy
is going crazy.

We have to stop.

There's no sign about dogs not being allowed,
so we can sit beside the water and listen, and
remember.

Years ago we carried the baby in a Moses
basket onto the beach. She was so small, a woman
sitting under a gigantic hat thought that she was
a doll.

I remember that I covered her tiny feet in the
sand, and she gave her first real baby smile.

I remember that she made happy baby noises
when we both took her into the warm waters of
the Gulf . . . and the water was warm and the sky
a fierce blue.

I knew she'd always love the water.

And at the same time in Ohio . . .

Shoogy and Bobby play cards on the blanket
while I take Feather into the water.

One minute I'm standing Feather up in a little
tide pool, the next—I'm in a dream and the baby
is me. The sky is bluer, and the water warmer. . . .

part three

beauty

Shoogy says that once she had a screaming, crying fit in front of five hundred people on the pageant circuit.

Her momma always sat in a certain place—to the right and four rows back. She'd get one of the spectators to move or she'd make sure she got to the seat first.

Shoogy says she always counted on her momma being right there.

But when it came time for her to go out onstage and sing, for the talent part of the show, she couldn't find her momma. She stalled and looked everywhere. Finally she just gave up and lay down on the stage and started crying. She was six.

She was in a few more contests, but one day her momma found her in the kitchen slicing her thigh with a fork. The next time she had cut off all her hair with nail clippers. She said it took her a couple of hours. Her momma had thought she was taking a nap.

I don't think I'm going to have a screaming fit.

But lately, all of a sudden, my head will start hurting, and I can feel my whole body get so stiff, I feel like it's going to break apart.

I've been slamming a lot of doors lately, too. Momma hasn't said anything yet, but I know she wants to.

When I try to think about Jack my head hurts even more. After I told Shoogy about my parents and how I'm feeling, she said she had something to clear my head.

We're sitting on the walkway of the town water tower, swinging our legs over the side. Green treetops and electric lines lie under us. Shoogy lights up a cigarette she stole from her momma's desperate pack. It's the pack she keeps in the garage when she's about to go out of her mind. She quit smoking a year ago and still needs to know she can get to cigarettes real fast if she has to.

Makes me like Mrs. Maple a little bit more knowing she isn't so perfect.

I say, "Why don't we just go over to the high school and light up some of the jocks' sweaty socks and inhale them?"

Shoogy just laughs and inhales a few more times. "Do you remember anything about your uncle Jack—or your dad or whatever it is you are calling him."

I look over the treetops. "I don't remember anything. Except a couple of days ago at the lake, I think I dreamed something—that didn't really happen."

Since I didn't say anything else, neither did Shoogy. I liked that about her. Most people didn't 'cause she usually got quiet just before she did something crazy.

"What if I jump from this? Do you think I could make it to the treetop over there by the old town hall?"

I look where she's pointing and nod my head. "I hope you take your cigarette when you go."

Shoogy puts the smoke out and stands up on the walkway and howls.

"Hey! Shut up, they're going to find us up here."

But she keeps on howling, and I notice for the first time the deep gashes on her thighs, right over her rain boots. I watch her howl over the trees, over the wires, past the plane flying overhead, and away from Heaven.

Shoogy stops howling and looks at me. "Don't you need to howl? Howl at the people who screwed you over."

I shake my head and say, "Howl for me."

And she does. . . .

The red lights that surround the tower have lit up. Shoogy pulls out a sandwich and hands me half. We sit eating and watching Heaven light up through the trees.

I lean back against the H painted on the tower.

"I always wanted to go live with my uncle Jack when I was little."

Shoogy says, "Sounds like he has a cool life. Never staying in one place too long. Living out of a pickup, moving around with his dog. What did you say his name was?"

"Boy."

"Boy?"

"Yeah, him and Pops have had a lot of dogs named Boy. It's this thing they got for the name."

"Maybe you could still go live with him."

"Why would I want to go live with another liar, girl? It'd be just like where I am now. Living with people who lie."

Shoogy tosses the crust of her bread over the side. "Oh."

"Living with people who lie to you . . . and here I am thinking how I got everything okay at home.

I mean, I like my family. Look at you, you can't stand to breathe the same air as yours."

"Thanks for reminding me."

"Well, it's true."

Shoogy gets up and leans over the railing. "I think I see the floodlights from my backyard. My dad thought it would keep burglars out, but all it does is stay on all night. The raccoons play under it."

I say, "Thugs, here?" How would they find their way out to sell the yard sheep and pink flamingos?

Shoogy yawns. "Yeah."

I finish the last of my sandwich and watch as Shoogy walks around the whole tower. I can only hear her as she comes around the back, hitting the side. When I first saw the water tower, I'd told Pops that it looked like E.T.'s head. He laughed and told everybody what I had said.

I stand up and scream, "Hell," for about two straight minutes until my voice is about gone.

Shoogy just looks at me while I'm screaming, and even through the shadows I see a smile on her face.

"What is it about being high up that makes you want to scream?" I say.

"I guess up this high you really think some-body might hear you. I mean, they'll stop what they're doing, look up, and say, 'Hey, man! What's up with that screaming? It must be somebody in trouble. It must be somebody real.'"

I look at Shoogy in her dark glasses at night. "Do you feel real?"

"What's real?"

"I don't know anymore, I guess. It all got pulled away from me. What if *everything* Lucy and Kevin have been telling me all these years has been one fat lie? I can't trust anything they say now, can I?"

Shoogy shrugs and says, "I wouldn't trust 'em."

I say, "You're right. Who would trust them?

"Want to go to Montana? I read this book about this woman who goes there. I mean, she almost froze to death there. . . ."

There's a red glow coming from Shoogy's mouth, and smoke circling us. She says, "You want to go someplace where some woman almost froze to death?"

"Yeah, but it was real. She did it. She did it by herself."

"What's the big deal? Did she fly?"

"No, she rode a horse to Montana from

Philadelphia back in the 1850s."

"I guess that's keepin' it real."

I say, "I hate this 'keepin' it real' stuff. What's it all about, anyway? Real *is* what is. If you have to keep something the way it is, then it's not going with the natural flow. That's lying. I mean, if you can't change because you think this is the way it always was and anything else would be phony, that's stupid.

"I'm pissed at my par—Kevin and Lucy. That's real. The way I'm dealing with it is real. I mean I can't just say, I understand why you both lied to me for a crillion years. Yeah, everything's cool. I can't talk about it. It's too stupid and it hurts me too much. That's real."

Shoogy laughs. "I was just agreeing with you about the woman going to Montana. That's all."

I start laughing, too. "Sorry."

Shoogy says, "Yeah."

I watch the shadow of Shoogy. Then I say, "Do you think Jack would have kept me if I was beautiful?"

Shoogy throws her cigarette over the side of the tower, then puts her arm around me. "We're all beautiful—so who knows why he did what he did."

full

$\mathcal{I}$ wake up, surprised, to a cardboard box at my feet and wonder if it was Momma or Pops who put it here. It's one of those flowered storage boxes about the size of a shoe box that people put letters in.

I wake up easy, you know, and I don't know how . . . I must be real tired. So tired, I didn't hear them come in.

It's been that way lately—me sleeping till somebody has to bang on my bedroom door. Butchy usually comes in and hits me with a pillow. Momma knocks hard and says, "Up, girl," which makes me think of dog tricks. Pops just knocks and says softly, "Marley." Softly, "Marley."

I love the sound of my name now. Want to hold on to it and hear people say it over and over again. I never heard the sound of my own name coming out of me. I say my name a lot now. It holds me somewhere I used to be. It makes me feel whole and full.

I like that they named me after Bob Marley.

Pops used to dance me around the house when I was little to his music. He used to dance me around . . . I'll never dance with him again.

Sleeping late is about not going down to breakfast and not saying the wrong thing. Not screaming, "LIARS." Not saying, "Was it worth it—making me so miserable now? Making me want to know why—and nobody can tell me."

Oh yeah, they can tell me that my mother really died. When I ask how—they just say she died and my dad, Jack, wasn't able to take care of me. Had too much sorrow in his soul and had to go away.

I know a lot of people with sorrow in their soul. Ma down at the Superette's got it. Why else would she keep that store open like she does? Never leaving it. Only stopping to get down on her knees and pray.

When I was little, I used to wonder if she put the Bible underneath her knees to cushion the pain from the old oak floors she was so proud of. I wondered if she'd lost a child or if her pain was that she never had one.

Sometimes when I was wiring money to Uncle Jack, I wondered if Ma made enough money at the

Superette. The only person she had to help her was her nephew, Chuck. He was this biker who grew tomatoes and liked to hang out at the Old Towne Tavern. He's the only person I ever saw help Ma at all.

Chuck was better than a son to Ma and he wasn't her blood son. Ma seemed to smile only for him . . . and I could almost believe that you could love a niece or nephew as much as a son or daughter. Almost.

Ma had sorrow.

But I'll bet a whole bunch of money and anything that's important to me that she wasn't leaving kids for other people to raise.

I kick the box with my foot, and it falls over the side of the bed and hits the floor. I lie on my back and stare up at the stars on my ceiling. At night they glow in the dark.

Every year Pops replaces the ones that fall off or just don't glow like they used to. He put my stars up when we first moved to Heaven. I can remember telling everybody I met that I had stars in my bedroom. Then one day he put the moon there for me.

The stars and the moon.

My Pops would stand underneath them with

me and look up at them like it was the first time he'd ever seen anything so pretty.

I'd do the same thing he did. Pointing at the stars. Remembering if he'd put them in the same place as the last time.

He was never wrong. The stars always stayed in the same place. I have to remember that. I have to keep on thinking about that when I want to scream at Momma, Pops, and Jack.

Heaven is in a valley surrounded by farms and woods. There's a million places to go if you want to be alone and all of them are within walking distance.

I walk through the kitchen, and Butchy is washing dishes. Pops and Momma are gone to work. I turn back toward the fridge and grab some grapes out of a bowl.

Butchy tosses soap bubbles at the window. He says, "What's up?"

"Nothing."

"What's that?" he says, pointing at the cardboard box.

"Something I haven't opened yet. Something Momma or Pops left in my room."

"What is it?"

"It says 'Baby Monna' on the box."

Butchy goes and sits at the kitchen table and looks scared. "You gonna open it now?"

Butchy hasn't been saying too much since I found him looking for his birth certificate in Momma and Pop's room. When he's around me he smiles. He always starts to say things to me but in the end always says, "Never mind."

He sits at the table banging a spoon. He's got his knee pads on already. He's been living on his board a whole lot more these days.

I saw him yesterday hiking up by Caveman Hill.

I went there once with him and his friends. Skinny boys with long shirts and baggy khakis. All of them looking for the perfect wave.

Caveman Hill will never be the ocean, but it slopes and dips through old twisted trees and burnt-out fields. Any minute you think you might see dinosaurs coming out of the dark night, getting in the way of the skinny boys on flying wheels.

I take a seat beside Butchy and shake my head. "I'm not opening anything now."

"What do you think is in there?"

I lay my head down on the table and close my eyes.

"You don't have to talk about it, Marley. I mean, after they told me, nobody's saying anything."

"It's all changed now. I still love you, but you aren't my brother. And at least if they'd lied to you, I'd still feel the same about you, because then you'd be going through these changes, too."

Butchy gets up, lets all the water out of the sink, and turns on the radio. He picks up the skateboard leaning against the pantry door and stands up on it.

He rolls out the back door, then stops. "We'll always be who we were to each other." Then he's gone to find the perfect wave.

Walking around town, I think about how the colors of everything have changed and it's like nobody has seen it happen.

They still put vegetables outside the Hahn Market.

Spin More Records still plays hip-hop on Saturday afternoons through the outside speakers, and classical music on Sunday mornings.

It's just that nobody has seen that the vegetables aren't as red or green as they used to be. The big album outside the record store is gray now instead of coal black. Nothing is as clear as it used to be.

⌒

I've been walking around town all day with this box in my hand. The cardboard is wet. I spilled a cherry Slurpee on it earlier. I almost left it on the bench in front of the hardware store where I watched Chuck, Ma's nephew, delivering tomatoes to different people on the block.

He has boxes and boxes of tomatoes in the back of Ma's Superette pickup truck. His arms flex his tattoos when he picks the boxes up. His smiling face says he planted and took care of these and now he'll feed everybody.

I don't notice him walking toward me. He stands there in a Harley T-shirt and work pants. Then he hands me a tomato almost as big as my head, and walks away.

I hold it, then put it on top of the box and look away. I think about Chuck and Ma, and when I look at it again, it's the reddest tomato I've ever seen in my life. Right there on Center Street. Right there beside me.

water

My Dear Sweet Marley,

The other day Boy and I stopped at the most incredible lake I've ever seen. I've seen some strange things, so believe me when I say this was one of the strangest.

In the middle of miles of wheat and other things being farmed, I came upon a lake with a beach surrounding it. The beach was surrounded by a wheat field. If I hadn't been in the pickup and a bit raised off the road, I never would have seen it.

Boy must have sensed it, though. He loves water and always knows when it's close.

The beach. What can I say about the beach? There it was, where it was. . . .

I've never seen such happy people. They were farm people who worked hard from sunup to sundown, and you could tell that when it was time for fun, they knew how to have it.

Maybe it just seemed to me that they didn't take the water for granted. All those wheat *fields and never-ending plains. You can see forever on the plains, Marley.*

Some people say farming gets in your blood. They say that about fishing and hunting, too. I guess it all has something to do with controlling the natural world.

But you really can't control nature, Marley. You can reel her in and plow her and even kill a few of her creatures. In the end you can kill everything she offers or you can take what she gives you.

It's important to understand the natural world.

Anyway, Boy and I sat on the beach, walked the beach, waded in the water, and generally people-watched — kids running around not minding their parents and parents running after them or reading under beach umbrellas and relaxing behind dark glasses.

A funny thing happened while we were checking out the scene on Starlight Beach. Great name, huh? I asked a man selling ice cream why it was called Starlight Beach and he said, "Why not?" I liked that answer.

Oh yeah, the funny thing. Boy started following a group of kids around and wouldn't leave them. Even when they went on the far side of the beach to play their boom boxes, he followed. I let him go 'cause they seemed to enjoy his company as much as he did theirs.

He especially liked a baby one of the kids was carrying around, probably his little sister. Boy always stayed at the baby's side. The baby, of course, would pull his ears and sit on him, but he didn't seem to mind. He stayed right there while the kids danced the afternoon away in the sand.

It reminded me of something from a long time ago.

Boy cried when it was time to leave. He whined and wouldn't come to me in the beginning, but in the end he trotted past the sand castles and picnic baskets, through the fields of wheat, and got in the truck.

I felt bad for him as we pulled away from Starlight. He looked out the back window for miles. I guess he was hoping the kids would follow.

Sometimes, Marley, I worry that I'm not being fair to Boy. He's never lived anywhere more than a few months. Maybe he needs a yard and a house, where he always knows

*where his water dish will be. I know having
one vet wouldn't mean anything to him, 'cause
he hates them all, but maybe it would be
easier. . . .*

*Maybe someday I'd like to know where my
water dish will be, too. . . .*

Peace and love from me and Boy,

Love to your folks and brother

*P.S. Thank you for all the dog drawings.
I think it's great of your friend Bobby to give
you lessons. I've papered most of the inside of
the truck with them. Boy is fascinated. He
gets real low on his belly and paws at the one
you did on yellow paper. Remember it? You
stamped thunderbolts all around the edges of
the paper.*

the next door

Once I heard Momma and Pops talking about a woman who used to work out of town and could only come back to Heaven on weekends. The woman had a baby that she used to leave with a sitter. The woman came home one weekend, and the sitter and her baby were gone.

She never saw her little boy again.

I was so little when I heard the story that I can't remember the name of the woman or if she still lived in Heaven. I just remember that I never wanted a baby-sitter.

Used to run screaming after Momma if she tried to leave me with one. Butchy used to follow me, saying, "It's okay, Marley, Momma's comin' back." He always said the same thing. Every time. He was younger than me, so how did he know?

How did he know?

Well, I guess he didn't know. Not only did my mother not come back, but another one took her place and didn't tell me that she wasn't the real one. I look at Momma and want her to be mine, really mine.

I feel bruised and motherless, even when I want to go to Momma lately and tell her it's okay. I just want what I used to have. But I can't. My legs won't carry me to her.

I miss her.

I put Uncle Jack's letter where I keep the others. I look in the bottom of the chest of drawers and run my hand through what seems like thousands of envelopes; all different colors and addresses. Some are written on motel stationary, and others were recycled from other people's mail.

I've been getting letters from Jack since I was a baby. Pops used to read them to me then. I learned to read when I was four—so Jack wrote them to me after that. I used to keep the letters in my toy box. Then I kept them in a Tinkertoy box, until it got too small.

I put the cardboard box in my letter drawer before I go to sleep. Unopened.

After carrying the box around for a few days, I got this idea that if I just threw it away, everything would go back to the way it was.

At Bobby's house, Feather uses it as a drum. She beats her baby hands on it and drools.

Bobby stands against his purple wall. "I'll stay with you while you open it."

I smooth Feather's soft hair and say, "That's okay."

"You not going to open it *ever*, then?"

"I don't know," I say.

Bobby goes into the kitchen and comes back with lemonade in tall, icy glasses. He says you can work through anything with something cold to drink in your hands.

He sits down cross-legged, and Feather crawls to him, begging lemonade. He lets her have a drop, and she puts baby floaties into his glass. He smiles.

"Why did your folks just drop this box off in your room? Didn't they want to be with you when you opened it? We're talking heavy stuff."

I take a gulp of lemonade and walk over to the window. A woman is dragging a huge picture down the street. I can't see what the painting is, but she's having a hard time with it. The door to Canvas opens, and the owner runs out and helps the woman get the painting inside.

"I don't know what to say to them, Bobby. I don't know whether to cuss 'em or hug 'em. I don't know whether to scream at them or stop talking to them. I think they know that, and that's why they're leaving me alone."

Bobby gives Feather another drop of lemonade before she crawls away from him and tries to take her diaper off. I look at her and wonder if my . . . Jack ever held me the way Bobby holds Feather.

Bobby gets up and goes to a canvas he's painting and turns it upside down.

"Don't say anything, then, 'cause you might say something that you'll regret saying. I know about that."

I walk across the white painted wood floor and stand next to Bobby. He doesn't talk about his life before coming to Heaven. I know he lived in Brooklyn and that he doesn't say that he misses it, but I can feel that he does. He's never talked about Feather's momma, but I feel like he misses her, too.

Must be sad to miss so much.

Must be sad to not know that you ever had anything to miss. Walking around in the world thinking you know it all. Thinking you know who you are. Walking around in the world like me.

Bobby's dreads brush my face.

He whispers, "When you're ready to open the next door to your life, I'll be there, if you want."

I lean against my friend, who's only a few years

older than me and has a baby and some secrets of his own. I lean against him harder and watch the box a few feet away that might tell me secrets of its own.

Feather finds it again and this time she chews on a corner. When she's had enough of that she beats on it again and smiles a slobbery grin at me and Bobby.

I flash again on me and Pops washing his car. He is still grinning at me, but Momma has come into the picture this time. She's got a camera and she's saying, "Give Momma a smile, baby. Give Momma a smile."

Shoogy is in my room when I get home. She says the door was open and nobody answered, so she came on in.

"I like your stars," she says.

I put my box on the dresser and fall across the bed beside her. "You say that every time you come in my room."

She taps the side of her sunglasses and picks at some lint on my bedspread.

"I wanted stars like yours, but my mother said it didn't go with the decor."

"The what?"

"You know—the bears and other woodland creatures in *my* room that *she* decorated."

Shoogy pulls off her rain boots and throws them across the room. I see some of the same scars around her ankles that I saw on her thigh the other day.

I say, "You're not a bear kind of person. What's up with that, anyway?"

Shoogy goes over and turns on my radio to a hip-hop station and says she likes my Zora Neale Hurston poster.

She falls down on my beanbag chair and takes out a cigarette.

I say, "Not here, girl."

"Sorry."

She puts the pack into her rain boots and leans back to listen to the music.

Shoogy looks over at my poster.

"No, guess I ain't a bear kind of person, but I sure come from a bear kind of house. You're lucky. Your mom and dad pretty much leave you alone. They don't want you to be something you're not."

I look at Shoogy like she's nuts, but see that she's for real. She sees my parents like that. And I know I used to see them the same way. I remember that. It hasn't been that long.

"That box over there is what I am. They kept that from me long enough, don't you think?"

Shoogy stretches her legs out and looks up at the stars.

I look at the scars on her brown legs and then look up at my stars, too.

The stars were a good thing, and I could look around the room and see other good things. Something unseen made Shoogy do what she did to herself, but I'd never felt that kind of pain before with Momma and Pops. I'd only felt pain after I didn't know where I stood or who I was.

Shoogy gets up and tosses the box onto the bed beside me. I look up at her frosted lips and dark spy sunglasses. She kneels on the floor beside the bed as I open the box on the same spot where I found it.

momma

Shoogy told me when I first met her that she used to cut herself so it would block out pain. I didn't understand. She told me that she couldn't cut deep enough. I almost cried when she said that. And I wondered what could have hurt her heart so much.

We're both fourteen. We both like the same music and think the same things are funny. . . .

I open the box by ripping off tape and untying a thin pink ribbon that's been wrapped around it. Inside there's another box. The top of it says, AKNOCKMAN'S SHOE STORES, MONTGOMERY, ALABAMA. There's a piece of tissue paper covering everything except a tiny baby shoe.

Who I was sat in front of me.

Shoogy takes off her sunglasses and holds on to my arm.

She says at her old school there was this boy who made up this song called "Black Girl with Violet Eyes." Her violet eyes look at me, then the box.

My baby shoes are pink.

I lift out a tiny white sweater with pink roses stitched in and a tiny hat to match it all. Next comes a hospital bracelet with the name FLOYD, MONNA typed in on the space under NAME; mother's name CHRISTINE FLOYD. I hold on to it.

Then I close the box. There's more, but I can't look at it. I hold on to the sweater, hat, and shoes. I hold on to the bracelet and curl up on my bed.

Evening sounds wake me up, and Shoogy is asleep on the floor. We've both been covered with cool cotton blankets, and I can smell Momma's perfume in the room. The baby clothes and bracelet are still in my hands.

I walk Shoogy home, and a bunch of little kids in Halloween masks come running at us from the direction of the Community Center. They're having Halloween in July. All the kids probably have five pounds of sugar in each of them. Shoogy stares at the hundreds of little kids dressed as ghosts or butlers with axes through the heart as they run down the street.

She does a cartwheel right in front of Ma's Superette and screams, "It's just like Christmas!"

I listen to the kids laughing and watch the way Shoogy looks, like she wants to go running after them.

In front of the Center, sombody's cut up a watermelon like a jack-o'-lantern, and there's lots of kids and parents sitting around eating sweet corn and hot dogs.

Shoogy decides to join in, and by the time I turn around and look back down the street, she's having Halloween in July with the rest of Heaven.

I walk back toward Riverview and twirl the baby bracelet in my pocket and feel better than I've felt in a couple of weeks.

Pops is sitting in the driveway as I come down the walk, still in the car wearing his work clothes.

Pops works in the lumberyard or, as he says, cuts wood for a living. "Cutting wood and wood-cutting," he always says. He says his job is what he does, not what he is. I asked him once what he was. He said the world's most famous thinker who hasn't been discovered yet. Then he laughed.

Pops leans out the car.

"Want to go for ice cream, kid?"

"Lactose intolerant," I say, and walk on by.

"They got Tofutti," Pops says, drumming on

the steering wheel. I look at his round face and the wood chips in his hair, then go around the front of the car and hop in.

Pops pulls the Impala out of the drive and heads out of town.

"Aren't we going to the Dairy Queen?"

Pops stops at a crosswalk to let some masked kids cross the street.

He puts in a tape.

"You know what song this is?" he says.

I know it's jazz, but I don't know the name of the song. I just look out the window and watch all the fields and cows blow by.

"Miles Davis. Nobody like him, Marley. Nobody ever will be. . . . "

"Do you look like my father?" I say as the fields and barns outside of Heaven blur into one.

Pops turns off the music and looks at me.

He pulls at the name tag on his shirt. I have all of his old shirts. Every time he gets new ones, I grab the old ones. I like the way they feel big and baggy on me. They're all I'd wear if I could.

"The last time I saw Jack, we did look alike. He's taller and has bigger ears." Pops laughs at some joke only he and Jack would get.

"Why?"

"Why what, Marley?" Pops slows the car down a little and reaches out to touch my arm. I move closer to the door, but not before I see the look in his eyes. It's like I just shot him.

"Why is this happening? Why didn't anybody tell me? You should have told me you all were raising me 'cause my mom was dead and my dad didn't want me. You should have told me when I was little."

Pops keeps driving and staring straight ahead. "Yeah, we should have told you when you were little, but not the things you think we should have."

I start kicking the passenger door. "Yeah, like you told me about magic and how one day I wouldn't mind having a brother."

Pops's voice gets real low. "Was I right about any of it?"

"I don't know anymore. Maybe the one big lie makes everything a lie."

Pops says, "Maybe. Maybe it does."

Pops used to do magic tricks for me and Butchy when we were little. I just naturally thought most kids grew up with their dad pulling rabbits out of hats and making vases and things disappear. When Butchy was real little Pops even made him disappear out of a hatbox.

I thought he could do anything.

One spring morning when I was five, me and my dog Holly were playing in the yard. A ball rolled out in the street, and Holly went after it. The lady in the station wagon never saw her.

I found out later Holly had probably died on the spot, but I didn't know that. I kept crying for Pops to make her come back. To make her stand up. Neighbors all around; and me screaming and hanging on to him.

Wanting magic and knowing he could get it for me.

Pops pulls over to the Tastee-Freeze on Route 306. A waitress comes over to the car to take our order. She smiles and pulls at her polyester uniform. I feel bad for her in the heat and sticky dress, so I order food and ice cream. Pops just orders ice cream and doesn't eat it when it comes.

We head home and don't say anything to each other.

When we drive by the YOU ARE ENTERING HEAVEN sign, Pops says, "It's always good to know where you are, I guess."

I move over closer to Pops. I say, "Sometimes I don't have a clue."

Pops says, "Sometimes it's easy to tell where you are. Just look around and notice the people who have always been there for you, and follow them."

I look out the window as we pass a poster on a telephone pole that says, SOUTHERN CHURCHES ARSON RELIEF.

Then I watch the last of the Halloween kids running home out the rear window of the Impala.

part four

love letters

$\mathcal{A}$ note I wrote to Jack.

> *Jack,*
> *Do you think about me like I'm your*
> *daughter?*
> *Do you think about me like that at all?*
> *Marley*

Then I tore it up.

Hadn't been down to wire Jack money in weeks.
Mom and Pops stopped asking, and I stopped
wanting to. Butchy does it now.

He wanted to know how we could give Jack so
much money. So he asked. Pops seemed surprised,
but told him.

And this is what Butchy told me. . . .

My mom, Christine, died in a car accident, and
it looked like the car company was at fault. Jack
got a lot of money. He got so much of it that it
kind of freaked him out, so he put it all in the

bank and let Pops deal with it.

Butchy says Pops told him he thought it was strange that neither he nor I had asked before. Butchy said he didn't ask 'cause he never thought about it. I just thought my parents loved Jack, and would give him anything. That's just me not knowing about money.

Butchy says Pops told him it all just like that, and I'm thinking to myself how easy it all would have been to tell me in the beginning. Just like that.

Alone in my room again, I open the Baby Monna Box.

Beside my baby clothes is a diamond ring in a velvet box and some letters Christine had written to Jack. I haven't read any of them yet. But written on the top of the envelope are the words LOVE LETTERS.

Bobby says people don't write love letters anymore. He says it's old-fashioned but kind of beautiful. Most people just go on the Net and e-mail who they love. I kind of think Bobby is old-fashioned in a way, that's why he knows. . . .

love letters. . . .
love letters. . . .

love letters. . . .
love letters. . . .

Petals fall out of the first letter. Just fall out and blow all around my room 'cause a breeze comes out of nowhere and carries the dark yellow flowers all over the place.

Christine liked yellow flowers. . . .

I am Christine's daughter, so that must be where I got my love of flowers.

The woman who digs in the yard now is my mother. Is not my mother. Is my mother. Is not my mother who I got my love of flowers from. She is not the woman who loved Jack, then died, and left him with a little baby. Me.

The hands I look at now are not the hands of the woman who digs in the yard. That can't be.

My mother is the woman who wrote love letters to my father who is not the man who works at the lumberyard and loves ice cream.

It's starting to be real 'cause there are love letters.

mountains

Today I put every penny I had into the church relief can at Ma's. I stuffed dollars bills into the can until Ma reached over and gently pulled my hands away.

Mrs. Maple broke her ankle playing tennis and had walked on it half a day before Shoogy's dad finally picked her up out of the front yard, put her in the car, and took her to the hospital.

The Caddy screeched down the road with the twins running behind it like their parents were never coming back. They walked back to the driveway holding hands.

Shoogy goes over and wraps her arms around them and it's the first time I ever saw her even seem like she cared for anybody who was related to her. The twins look at her and smile, then walk back to the house. Still hand in hand.

Shoogy sits down on the front yard beside me and pulls up big handfuls of grass and throws them up in the air. "She's always been like that," she says.

"Who and like what."

Shoogy lays back on the beautiful grass. She pulls out a piece of clover. Our yard is full of both of them.

"My mom is something. She never has pain or problems. Some people would call that perfect."

"Your mom's scary 'cause she doesn't complain?"

Shoogy rolls over on her stomach and pulls up more grass.

Shoogy says, "I'll never be like her."

She says it real sad, though, and that surprises me. I mean, Shoogy is beautiful like her Mom and everything. It's funny, 'cause I didn't think she cared to be like anybody in her family. The perfect Maples. Shoogy wanted to be a perfect Maple?

I start to see her differently.

I start to think it doesn't just roll off her back since she stopped cutting herself 'cause she couldn't be perfect.

The twins are running out the front door toward Shoogy.

I say, "Later."

Shoogy waves and puts one of the twins on her back. She gives him a horseback ride until they both fall on the ground laughing. . . .

I almost run into Pops as he's coming out of Ma's. He should be at work, but there he is munching on chips and sucking on a juice box like it's something he always does in the middle of the day. I get a hit of cool breeze from the air-conditioning coming out of Ma's. Pops smiles at me and offers me a chip.

We walk over to a bench outside of Ma's and sit down.

Pops says, "Had a few errands to run, so I took the afternoon off. So this is what it feels like to hang out in the middle of the day?"

"Yep, I guess this is it."

I look up the street. The music store is getting a piano delivered, and a woman pushing a stroller walks past singing a lullaby. Two doors down, the bookstore is having their windows cleaned.

"Guess I haven't missed much. What's up with you? Doing anything fun?"

"I thought I'd go over and pick up Feather. Bobby's working at home today. He's painting small signs, so Feather's probably covered in paint by now."

Pops hands me another chip. "You're a good friend, Marley."

I look at Pops as he finishes his drink box. He looks far away from Center Street and Heaven. He could be off in the mountains somewhere. He could be sitting on top of the highest mountain in the world.

"What were you doing at Ma's?"

"Errands."

"What kind of errands?"

Pops laughs. "Errands I can't do if I'm working."

"I could have done them for you."

"You going to keep bothering me? Is it that you have too much free time, or do you really care about the things I have to do?"

I laugh and say, "The first one."

I get up to go. Pop scrunches up his drink box and throws it in the trash can by the bench.

"Say hi to Bobby for me. Hi to Feather, too."

I look at Pops still sitting on the bench. He's gone back to the mountains.

Mr. and Mrs. Maple wave to me as they pass me in their car. A second later Mr. Maple has backed the car up and is smiling at me. I go over to the car. Mrs. Maple has a cast on her leg and is smiling like her husband.

Mr. Maple says, "We're having a cookout

tomorrow. Hope you can come."

"Yeah, I can come. Shoogy invited me this morning."

Mrs. Maple leans toward her husband. "Glad she did."

Mr. Maple waves another car around.

I just notice that the Maples are wearing the same tennis outfits. Mrs. Maple doesn't look like a person who just broke her ankle. Her hair is in a perfect bun.

She says, "I'm glad our daughter found you. It's hard for her to make friends."

I start to feel real uncomfortable in the middle of the street. I start to think the smiling Maples are going to have me for lunch. I guess my eyes are getting to look like a deer caught in the head-lights, 'cause Mr. Maples says, "I guess we should be on our way. I haven't been into work today. Looks like a half day off is going to turn into a whole day."

I say, "Yeah, everybody's taking off today."

They smile and drive off.

The twins will be glad to see them; maybe Shoogy will, too.

I'm starting to think the family thing isn't as clear as I thought. The Maples. I can't get past the fact that they really love Shoogy. Perfect looks, house, and all don't keep them from seeing who she is.

Mrs. Maple's eyes got all watery when she was telling me she was happy Shoogy met me. I wish I could dislike the Maples more. I tried for Shoogy's sake, and the scars on her legs. . . .

Every day it all gets more fuzzy around the edges about the people who call themselves our families. . . .

I think of Pops, in the mountains.

Feather is only painted a little when I get to Bobby's. Bobby sees me and gets that thankful look on his face, then kisses Feather as I take her out the door.

After a moment he runs out after me with her stuffed diaper bag, gives it to me with a kiss on the head, and goes back to work.

Feather and I sit awhile on the bench by Ma's and watch the world go by. I think about folks as Feather falls asleep, dreaming baby dreams, and it's like we're in the mountains, too.

pop!

*I*nstead of going to Shoogy's mom's picnic, I hang upside down in our maple tree out back eating Pop Rocks and thinking about how a lot of animals live their whole lives jumping around from tree to tree.

(Can't stand the thought of having too much fun. I feel too sad and shaky, so no picnic.)

I figure if I can stay up here a while, everybody will think I went to the picnic and leave me alone.

They're watching me, you know.

I started noticing it a few days ago. It's not only Mom and Pops watching me. Butchy is, too.

We'll be talking about something like skateboarding or comic books or how I'd been thinking about moving to Montana, and all of a sudden he's not talking anymore. He's watching me and waiting. For what, I don't know.

I think about it for a while and watch some squirrels on the ground looking up at me. I drop them a few Rocks and they sniff, then ignore them. I'm kind of glad they do, 'cause a squirrel eating Pop Rocks would not be pretty.

I guess if you think about it, a girl hanging upside down from a tree limb eating candy and getting paranoid about everything isn't that great, either.

Pop!

music

I feel a little better. It's three days after the Maples's picnic, and I think the tree helped—a little. I think sloshing my brains upside down for a couple hours knocked the cobwebs loose.

Feather and I had been listening to music all morning. By the time the sun got too hot, Feather started fussing, which isn't like her. She didn't eat her bananas and she wouldn't even clap when her favorite song came on the radio. So I figured I'd take her for a walk to Shoogy's house. I sang the Sunshine song all the way there. I messed the words up pretty bad, but Feather managed to bab-ble in tune.

The twins are spinning in circles and running into each other as I stroll Feather up the sidewalk to the front door of their house.

I watch the twins fall down screaming, and I say, "Is your sister home?"

They look at me and laugh like they don't have good sense.

When I ask again, they laugh even harder.

So I take Feather out of her stroller and open the front door to the Maples's house. Shoogy's sitting in the middle of the living room floor with her legs crossed and flute music on. I only want to stay a few minutes, so I sit Feather on the floor and she aims her baby head for a huge glass vase standing in the corner. She's speeding up to a fast crawl—she still gets everywhere quicker that way—when Shoogy leans over and grabs her and lets her play with the newspaper she pulls from underneath the throw rug.

"Your brothers are—"

Shoogy rolls onto her stomach. "Strange?"

"Yeah, I guess. But what I really wanted to say is that they don't seem to need anybody else, being twins and all."

"They don't."

Shoogy stretches out, and I can't help but look at the cuts on her legs. It still bothers me. She says it shouldn't. She says I don't let enough go. I feel too much. I need to learn to do something about it.

"You don't still do it, do you?"

Shoogy asks, "Do what?"

When I point to her legs, she looks at them like they just attached themselves to her.

Then Shoogy just smiles at me and says that

Feather has probably eaten the whole sports page. By the time I get to her over by the couch, she's grinning newsprint.

"Was it good, Feather?"

She keeps on grinning as I pull about a ton of paper out of her mouth. She decided to store the paper in her cheeks instead of swallowing it.

Shoogy gets up, turns the flute music off, and puts on some rap music just as her mom walks through the front door.

At first I think it's a coincidence, but the look on Shoogy's face tells me different. Mrs. Maples doesn't look like she'd appreciate rap. She looks crisp, like she just walked out of a magazine, like she probably always smells good and never sweats. She's perfect.

And talking to me and I'm not even paying attention.

"I saved some of it for you."

I say, "Excuse me."

Mrs. Maple sits down on the white couch with Feather in her lap. Somehow she's got Feather, and the baby isn't trying to run. She just looks up at Mrs. Maple and grins, then leans her head against her and falls asleep.

Mrs. Maple yells over the music that Shoogy's

being kind enough to share with the neighbors. My mom would have just cut me a real nasty look and the music would have been off, but that doesn't happen here.

Mrs. Maple screams, "The pie, I saved you some peach pie. Sugar said it's your favorite. It is, isn't it?"

I scream back at her, "No."

She yells back at me, "Good. I'm sorry you missed the picnic. Is your grandmother okay now?"

I look across the room at Shoogy, and she's about dead, laughing. I don't think I've ever heard her laugh so hard before. And Feather keeps on sleeping, drooling on Mrs. Maple, who keeps shaking her head and hollering at me that she's already started taking calcium because she doesn't want to have the problems my grandmother has when she gets older.

It's all too much to take about my nonexistent grandmother and peach pie. I smile at Mrs. Maple and take Feather off her lap, then shoot Shoogy a real dirty look and get out of there.

It gets weirder and weirder every time I go to Shoogy's house. You couldn't tell it by just looking at them, but the Maples are nuts.

And sometimes Shoogy can be mean.

As far as that goes—so can I. I think I have more reason than Shoogy does to be mean. It's hard for me, though. I don't think I'll ever be too good at punishing people.

I push Feather's stroller back toward her house, and we start to sing "Sunshine" when somebody rides past us in a pickup with their radio on playing Feather's favorite song. She starts to clap her hands and smile. We walk past the truck, which is just parked by the hardware store, and Feather points at the dog who leans out the passenger window and looks at us both like he knows us.

letters

On Sundays we always get in the car and go someplace we've never gone before.

Pops whines about filling the tank up, and Mom says as long as we don't go back to the place that was supposed to make the best omelettes in the world. She was sick for four days after eating there. Butchy puts on his headphones and make-believes he's boarding down a smooth mountain. I used to think about my uncle and mountains and the places he went to and the people he met. I'd think about him and Boy.

If you think about how things might have been a long time ago if something had just changed a little—you might just bug out.

What if Christine hadn't died?

I've been carrying Christine's love letter around with me. The petals are falling apart in my pocket. I feel better with it.

We missed the Sunday drive last week because of Christine's letter. I couldn't find it just as I was about to go out the door. I tore the house up.

When I finally looked up, everybody was standing around me looking at their feet or the wall.

I threw the rug in the corner of the room, slid to the floor, and cried.

My whole body ached like I'd been punched.

I sobbed, "I don't have that much, you know. I just got parts of her back. Just the paper parts. The parts with words and ink. The parts that can be folded and stored. Folded and lost . . . it isn't just paper to me now. It's like my mother was holding me in her lap and letting me have the necklace around her neck. It was something I could take away that was part of her. And, and . . . if I'd known. If you had only told me when I was little, it would all be okay. I know it would all be okay."

Momma knelt down next to me and covered me with her body.

My heart hurt so bad. I fell asleep on the floor.

When I woke up, Pop and Butchy were moving the TV—looking behind it. Mom was going through the bookshelves just in case . . . just in case.

Heaven
I'm in Heaven
and my heart . . .

A letter from Jack.

> Marley,
>
> Yesterday, Boy and I slept by a beautiful river. We had spent most of the day in the St. Louis. I checked out a baseball game. I got tickets in a trade from a man in Indiana who liked this blanket I'd bought in South Dakota.
>
> I thought about you as I sat by the river. I thought about what I would say to you—if I met you finally. I thought about how much you might look like Christine.
>
> Do you hate me, Marley?
>
> I was thinking yesterday by the river that if I was fourteen and lived in a small town and loved my family—I'd hate me.
>
> I have been worrying about it a lot. Boy knows something's wrong. He sticks close and watches me when I cross the street. He stays close when I sleep, too. I must have bad dreams, 'cause sometimes I wake and find him looking me right in the eye. What do you think?
>
> Incredible dog, or dog's hallucinating pal?
>
> Do you think there would ever come a time

> *when you think you might like to see me now?*
> *I know things have changed so much for you,*
> *me not being your uncle Jack anymore.*
>
> *I don't have to be your uncle, Marley; but*
> *I certainly won't ever try to be your dad. You*
> *have one who loves you, as I do. . . .*
>
> *Jack*
> *P.S. If you want to write me back, your*
> *dad knows where I'll be staying. He'll*
> *forward the letter to me.*

I wrote back.

> *Jack,*
> *I lost the petals and a love letter that used*
> *to belong to Christine.*
> *Marley*

Bobby asks me if I want to go to work with him. I can take Feather along and let her play while he works. He says he misses her in the daytime and just needs to look over and see her face. He says he'll pack a lunch for us tomorrow if it's okay with me. I tell him it is.

While I'm walking back home I can't help but think how Jack had stayed away all these years.

Hadn't he ever wanted to take me to work with him? See me in the daytime? Look at my face?

When I get home Momma is sitting on the front porch. When she looks up she's crying, and I run to her. Just as I'm about to get hysterical about Pops or Butchy she hands me Christine's letter. The envelope is a little dirty and looks like it had been chewed on, but the letter and petals are okay.

Momma wipes her eyes. "Found it under the tree out back."

I put the letter in my back pocket and sit next to Momma and notice I sit the same way she does, hunched over.

Then she says, "I loved your mom, Marley."

I nod my head and move closer to her. We wave away flies and watch the cars go by.

wings

Last night I dreamed everybody I knew had wings.

Mom and Pops had huge blue wings; Butchy had green ones. Feather had little orange wings that moved like a hummingbird's. Bobby and Shoogy were fixing each other's wings with paste which they didn't think would work.

But there I was—wingless, sitting on top of a plane waiting for takeoff. I was mad at everybody else 'cause they could fly anytime they wanted, and they were all saying wings aren't always as great as you think. Pops complained that you couldn't get a good middle seat at the movies, and Mom said they were hell in the office.

I woke up smiling.

There are yellow ducks on the tiles in Bobby's bathroom. While he's giving Feather a bath she's pointing at the ducks and quacking.

I close the toilet lid, sit down, and wait for Feather's bath to be over. I start to read some of the storybooks Bobby keeps in a basket in the bath-room.

And I remember.

She's singing a song while I splash bubbles all over the tub. Every few verses I look at her and laugh out loud, splashing the bubbles more. Soon we are both covered in bubbles. She's singing louder when all of a sudden, a wet, bubbly dog is in the tub with me and I am laughing, calling out his name.

"Boy, Boy, Boy, Boy. . . ."

Bobby's painting a billboard outside town for a farmer who has lived in Heaven for ninety-six years. The old man says he loves the town so much, he wants to give it a present.

Bobby's been painting the billboard for a few weeks. It sits on a hill in what used to be the farmer's cow pasture. He only keeps a few cows now, around the yard to remind him of what it used to be like.

We load Feather up in her car seat and head off into the warm morning.

Bobby says, "On mornings like this, I don't even miss the city or my family."

Since Bobby hasn't ever really talked about his

family that much, I'm a little surprised.

I say, "You've never really talked about too many people, Bobby."

He slows down near the river leading out of town to wait for a mama raccoon and her babies to cross the road. "Yeah, well, I got a few brothers."

"Parents?" I ask hopefully. I can't stand the thought of Feather not having grandparents any more than I can stand the thought of anyone not having parents. It makes my stomach hurt.

"Uh-huh. I got a mother and a father. They haven't been together since I was little—so I don't have parents. I got Mary and Fred."

Feather has fallen asleep in her car seat. Her little baby hands hold on to a stuffed duck with a really bent beak.

"Did you mind not having Mary and Fred together?"

Bobby laughs and waves to a man sitting on his porch smoking a pipe.

"Having Mary and Fred separately was more than any child could take. Mary is a photographer, and Fred is a chef. One was always dragging me off who knows where to get photo stories, and the other was always experimenting new recipes on me. I had an interesting childhood."

"Sounds great."

Bobby looks at me and smiles secretly. He always does it, and it makes me feel like I've missed something. "Isn't your life good?"

I say, "It was until a few weeks ago."

"Yeah, I see what you mean."

Bobby speeds up and flies by all the cornfields heading out of town.

When I was little, Mr. Calvin down the road used to threaten to put all us kids in the cornfields in the dark if we didn't stop running over his roses and peonies. We'd listen with our heads down and our hands folded in back of us. Then most of us would go home and have nightmares about corn monsters.

Mr. Calvin didn't have kids.

Pops said that to help me to understand why Mr. Calvin said the things he did to us. Pops always looked like he felt sorry for Mr. Calvin, childless and passing nightmares on to kids that weren't his.

Feather is still asleep as I carry her to the field with a blanket. Bobby carries his work things and the picnic basket. I lay Feather in the warm sun and watch her soft baby breathing. Bobby carries a ladder from behind the billboard, sets it up, climbs it, and takes off the huge tarp that has been covering his work.

Seconds later, I'm sitting in the morning sun looking at my dream . . . Bobby turns around once to me, smiles secretly again, then goes to work on the wings of a woman sitting on an airplane. . . .

ticket to heaven

Marley,

When you were a baby, I used to come into your room and sing to you. I'd sing from the radio. I'd make up songs and stay beside your crib until you would fall asleep. It got to the point where you wouldn't sleep until I sang.

Christine didn't think it was the best idea I ever had, 'cause I was the only one it worked for. What would happen, she said, if I wasn't able to be there for you some night? What if my work shift changed, or I had to be somewhere?

I kept telling myself that she was worrying for nothing. I'd be there forever. . . .

When you write me about your friends, it helps me feel better that you have found a family outside of your family. I feel I've not left you alone.

My brother, your dad, could not love you more. The same goes for your mom.

> *Even though they love you—I think it's*
> *time. I just decided to get a ticket to Heaven.*
> *A ticket to you.*
> *Love,*
> *Jack*

Shoogy was with me over by the park when I read the letter from Jack that said he had just bought a ticket to Heaven. . . .

Shoogy wonders why he isn't driving his truck or bringing Boy with him.

"I think he's speaking metaphorically."

Shoogy pushes her sunglasses up off her nose and sits with her back next to the park bench. There're hardly any kids in the park at all. It's quiet.

Shoogy leans toward me. "How do you feel, Marley?"

I look down the road leading past downtown then out of the village.

I say to myself, yeah—Marley, how do you feel? How do you feel?

Later that day, Pops says, "Do you mind that Jack is coming?"

We're sitting under the maple tree watching the sun go down.

"Who invited him, Pops?"

Pops watches the squirrels running up and down the picnic table.

"He invited himself. He wants to see you. He says it's time."

"Maybe he's wrong."

Pops puts his arm around me. "Maybe he's right."

When I was six, I got stuck in a snowdrift in our front yard. I remember I had painted a picture of some bears at school and I wanted to show my mom. I remember they were purple and orange and that I hadn't noticed that the snow was getting deeper as I ran slower and slower.

Finally, I was in the middle of the yard, stuck.

It seemed like I was stuck for an hour, but Momma said it was only a minute before she came out in a robe and Pop's tall fishing boots.

When I was warm and had shown my tear-streaked picture to Momma, she put it on the refrigerator and carried me into the living room. She sat me beside her on the couch and told me that I was okay and that she would always take care of me. That Pops would, too.

When he got home he dug out a trail from the middle of the yard. I watched him through the window from a chair.

After a while we laughed about me being trapped in the front yard. So close to home. I always laugh hardest at the story now, but I still don't walk through the front yard on snowy days.

Butchy's spinning 360s on the front sidewalk. He's moving to the music in his headphones, so I sit in the driveway and watch him do what he loves best. When he sees me watching him, he grins, but keeps on spinning. That's him.

I love Butchy.

He rolls over to me after a few minutes. "What, no applause?"

"I'm saving it up for your prime-time debut."

Butchy sits down beside me, and we roll his skateboard back and forth between us.

He says, "I thought you were supposed to be watching Bobby's kid today."

"Bobby took the day off to take Feather to the doctor for a checkup. It's not her favorite thing, and he said he liked me too much to put me through it."

"Yeah, guess you've been through enough the last few weeks."

"What? You worried about me?"

Butchy lowers his head and watches ants.

"I ain't worried. I just think about you sometimes. I just think about . . . "

"How I'm not your blood sister."

Butchy lays down flat on his back in the driveway and looks straight up. "It sucks."

I say, "Yeah, it does. Big time."

We both just let the idea that it sucks hang in the air. Wasn't much more to say about that part of it.

"Butchy, did you know Jack's coming here to meet me?"

Butchy looks at me like I just threw his skateboard in the river.

"He's not coming here?"

"Yeah, here."

"Marley, you aren't leaving with him or anything. I mean, you're ours. Not his."

"It's going to be okay. I mean—sooner or later."

Butchy jumps up and pulls me along with him. "Come on. Time for you to learn to ride."

Butchy runs in the house and brings out a helmet. I didn't even know he had one. Momma just gave up on him after a while. He used to tie it around his waist.

Butchy runs along beside me for a couple of blocks on the sidewalk. I do mostly what he tells me except for a couple of times I fall on my face and butt. In a few minutes we're at the edge of town, heading downhill. A few seconds later, I'm flying on wheels past trees and houses and a couple of dogs barking.

After that I'm lying in a big yard just as the sprinkler comes on. Butchy is beside me.

"So that's what it's like?"

Butchy opens his mouth to drink some of the sprinkler water. "Oh, yeah, that's just what it's like."

"Some life, brother."

The water keeps coming down, and the people who own the house watch us from their living room window.

Butchy takes the helmet and puts it over his eyes. I listen to the tap, tap of the water on the helmet and Butchy's muffled voice.

"Yeah, it's some life."

heaven

Momma said that it was destined we'd find Heaven. She said that postcard she found was supposed to be there. She believes in destiny and she says there isn't a damned thing any of us can do about it.

I believe I was destined to know the people I know and lose my mother in a car accident that wasn't supposed to happen. Jack was destined not to be able to stand any of it, and leave me.

Earlier today Shoogy, Bobby, and Feather showed up with a gallon of ice cream wearing cat masks left over from Halloween in July. We all sat in the backyard eating Rocky Road and collecting flies.

Nobody mentioned Jack. Bobby talked about going to the lake and getting a few buckets of sand for Feather. He didn't like the store-bought kind.

Shoogy said, "Let's go, cats." Hugged me and carried Feather to the car.

Bobby fed me a last spoonful of ice cream, then waved good-bye.

Mom, Pops, Butchy, and me sit in the living room and listen to the sounds of the summer. We try to talk to each other—to let each other know nothing is about to change.

Pops tells a joke.

We all laugh.

Mom tells a story about something that happened at work, and Butchy asks her if she thinks maybe some of the people in her office have too much free time. Mom says, "Definitely," and smiles.

It's like we're all strangers waiting for a bus at the station. Any minute somebody was going to ask somebody else to watch their iced tea so they could go to the bathroom.

A few minutes later, we're all laughing so hard at nothing that we don't hear the door slam in the driveway. And we don't see the man who looks like my dad and the dog who stands beside him watch us with a smile through the screen door.

There are 1,637 steps from my house to the Western Union in Heaven. I've walked by the playground, stores, and the coffee shop since I can remember. It was all old to me until I was suddenly pointing it all out to Jack, who quietly walked beside me with Boy.

I point out Ma's and say we should stop in— you can find anything you would ever need in there, and she wouldn't even mind having Boy come in.

Before we go in Jack looks through the window and asks, "They got Western Union?"

The question makes me smile.

Boy must already know the answer as he wags his tail and tries to nose his way in.

There's this sore part in my heart that isn't as aching as it was, so now I can smile about the Western Union. It hasn't been all that much time, either. I just don't hurt so much.

I don't want to hurt anymore. That's all.

I want to think about Momma and destiny, Pops, and how I got to see Jack's face all these years because of him.

My family is still just that—only the titles have been renamed. Butchy is still the boy I love, who rolls through life. Momma is still the one who digs and plants and does have hands that look like mine. And Pops is still the man who, when I close my eyes, I can see his smile.

~~~

I realized yesterday that a letter Jack sent last April was about me and Christine. We'd worn long dresses with sunflowers on them. He'd started telling me about my mother before I even knew she existed.

I watch Jack now as we all sit and talk in the backyard, across from the river. Jack laughs with Pops and Momma shakes her head when she spots a new scar on Butchy's knees from his skateboard.

For a split second everything is so normal and warm. It's almost perfect, like the day I sat in the field with Bobby, Shoogy, and Feather. I don't feel like I could ever love any of these people more than I do in that one moment.

Shoogy would call it a Hallmark moment, then light up a cigarette and say, "Forget it," but only so I wouldn't know how she really felt. Bobby would say, "The moment was what it was."

They'd both be so right.

A story Jack told me about my mother . . .

Christine had been afraid of storms her whole life. When I was born she decided she needed to get over that fear. How would she ever make me brave if I saw her fear the wind and the lightning?

In the middle of the night when I was eight days old, a storm came blowing across the countryside. Jack remembered how Christine shook as she picked me up and carried me, wrapped in my blanket, out to the front porch. He watched from the window as she sang to me on the porch swing and faced the storm down.

In the end she went to sleep with me in her arms. Perfect.

I dreamed of Christine after Jack told me that story. I dreamed of sunflowers and talking vegetarian dogs too. I loved dreaming about Christine, and I want her to know that I love the river that winds by my house.

That I love the people who raised me by that river, and that I love the man who finally came back to tell me the stories I needed to hear from so long ago.

Even though some of the stories will hurt my heart and sometimes make me afraid of losing more of what I have; I want her to know that it's been a fine life, for a girl like me, in Heaven.